Here's what kids have to say to
Mary Pope Osborne, author of
the Magic Tree House series:

*If you didn't make the Magic Tree House Books
I would go nuts!!!!*—Anthony

*Jack gave me the idea of getting a notebook
myself.*—Reid K.

*I hope that you make more Magic Tree House
books. They bring magic to my life.*
—Michell R.

*You gave me the courage to read. Thanks!*
—Lydia K.

*I like your books because they are very exciting.
It's like I'm traveling around the world with
Jack and Annie.*—Elizabeth C.

*Our imaginations are soaring thanks to you!*
—Julie M.

*Your books inspired me to read, read, read!*
—Eliza C.

*Reading your books gave me the idea to write
a book myself.*—Tyler

*I think your books are great. I can't sleep
without reading one.*—Leah Y.

# Teachers and librarians love Magic Tree House books, too!

*Your stories have been a very special part of every day in our class for the last two years. I read aloud to the class each day and we choose someone who gets to be "Jack/Annie," complete with backpack, glasses and journal. We have props from every book. . . . The children act out what is going on.*—L. Horist

*Introducing my students to your books is the best thing I've done. . . . Jack and Annie have incredibly helped my students' growth in reading.* —D. Boyd

*Thank you for these great books. They truly "light the fire within" that helps motivate students to read. I enjoy them myself!*—D. Chatwin

*It is refreshing as a classroom teacher to be able to use such interesting, informational adventure books to motivate and encourage good reading habits.*—R. Trump

*You have created a terrific tool for motivating children to learn about historical moments and places.*—L. George

*As a teacher I love how easily your books tie in with curriculum studies. Science and Social Studies units can easily be supplemented using your series. . . . Your books let my students experience other places and times beyond their front door.*—T. Gaussoin

*Due to your wide variety of settings, my students are learning an invaluable amount of information about history and the world around them, sometimes without even realizing it.*—L. Arnts

*It amazes me how these books easily lured my students into wanting to read.*—T. Lovelady

Dear Readers,

Last year, while my husband Will and I were doing research for our Magic Tree House Research Guide on rain forests, we visited the Bronx Zoo in New York. As we passed by the gorilla area, we saw a large gorilla sitting under a tree. She was staring very intently at us. We said hi to her—and she stuck out her tongue at us! I'm convinced she was just trying to make us laugh. And we did! In fact, we <u>still</u> laugh whenever we think about that moment.

We found out later that the gorilla's name is Pattycake. I keep a photograph of Pattycake on my desk, and I feel as if she's a giant, friendly spirit who overlooks all my work.

I love gorillas more than I can say. And I hope that by the time you finish reading <u>Good Morning, Gorillas</u>, you'll love them as much as I do.

All my best,

Mary Pope Osborne

# Good Morning, Gorillas

by Mary Pope Osborne

illustrated by Sal Murdocca

A STEPPING STONE BOOK™

Random House 🏠 New York

*For Dr. Michael Pope*

Text copyright © 2002 by Mary Pope Osborne
Illustrations copyright © 2002 by Sal Murdocca

www.randomhouse.com/magictreehouse

*Library of Congress Cataloging-in-Publication Data*
Osborne, Mary Pope.
Good morning, gorillas / by Mary Pope Osborne ; [Sal Murdocca, illustrator].
p.  cm. — (Magic tree house ; #26) "A stepping stone book."
SUMMARY: The magic tree house takes Jack and Annie to an African rain forest,
where the siblings encounter gorillas and learn to communicate with them.
ISBN 978-0-375-80614-8 (trade) — ISBN 978-0-375-90614-5 (lib. bdg.)
[1. Gorillas—Fiction. 2. Human–animal communication—Fiction.
3. Time travel—Fiction. 4. Magic—Fiction. 5. Tree houses—Fiction.]
I. Murdocca, Sal, ill. II. Title.  PZ7.O81167 Go 2002  [Fic]—dc21  2002017828

Printed in the United States of America  First Edition  July 2002
30  29

Random House, Inc.  New York, Toronto, London, Sydney, Auckland

# Contents

# Prologue

One summer day in Frog Creek, Pennsylvania, a mysterious tree house appeared in the woods.

Eight-year-old Jack and his seven-year-old sister, Annie, climbed into the tree house. They found that it was filled with books.

Jack and Annie soon discovered that the tree house was magic. It could take them to the places in the books. All they had to do was point to a picture and wish to go there. While they are gone, no time at all passes in Frog Creek.

Along the way, Jack and Annie discovered that the tree house belongs to Morgan le Fay. Morgan is a magical librarian of Camelot, the long-ago kingdom of King Arthur. She travels through time and space, gathering books.

In Magic Tree House Books #5–8, Jack and Annie help free Morgan from a spell. In Books #9–12, they solve four ancient riddles and become Master Librarians.

In Magic Tree House Books #13–16, Jack and Annie have to save four ancient stories from being lost forever. In Magic Tree House Books #17–20, Jack and Annie free a mysterious little dog from a magic spell. In Magic Tree House Books #21–24, Jack and Annie help save Camelot. In Magic Tree House Books #25–28, Jack and Annie learn about different kinds of magic.

# 1
## Dark and Rainy

*Tap-tap-tap.*

Jack sat up in bed. Rain tapped against his window. His clock said 5 A.M. It was still dark outside.

Annie peeked into his room.

"Are you awake?" she whispered.

"Yep," said Jack.

"Ready to find some special magic?" she asked.

"Maybe we should wait," said Jack. "It's so dark and rainy."

"*No* waiting," said Annie. "I'll get an umbrella. You bring a flashlight. Meet you downstairs."

"Okay, okay," said Jack.

He jumped out of bed. He pulled on his clothes and put on a jacket. Then he grabbed his backpack and flashlight.

Jack slipped downstairs and out the front door. Annie stood on the porch in jeans and a T-shirt. The air was chilly and breezy.

"Don't you need a sweater or something?" said Jack.

"I'm okay," she said. "Let's go."

Annie raised the umbrella. Jack turned on the flashlight. They followed a circle of rainy light down their street into the woods.

They headed through the Frog Creek woods. The flashlight lit up the trees—the

4

wet leaves and dark branches. Then it shined on a dangling rope ladder.

Jack raised the flashlight beam.

"There it is," he said.

A circle of light lit the magic tree house.

"Morgan's not there," said Annie. "I can tell."

"Maybe she left us a message," said Jack.

Jack grabbed the rope ladder and started up. Annie put the umbrella down and followed. When they climbed inside, Jack shined the flashlight around the tree house.

Morgan le Fay wasn't there. But the scrolls from their trip to old England were.

"Here's proof we found a special magic yesterday," she said.

"Yeah," said Jack, smiling. "*Theater* magic." He had great memories of acting in a play by their friend William Shakespeare.

"Did Morgan leave us a new secret rhyme?" asked Jack.

He shined the flashlight on a book lying under the window. A piece of paper was sticking out of the book.

"Yes!" said Annie. She picked up the book and pulled out the paper.

Jack shined his light on the paper while Annie read aloud:

*Dear Annie and Jack,*

*Good luck on your second journey to find a special magic. This secret rhyme will guide you:*

*To find a special kind of magic
in worlds so far apart,
speak a special language,
talk with your hands and heart.*

*Thank you,
Morgan*

"What kind of language does she mean?" Jack asked.

"I guess we'll find out," said Annie. "Where are we going?"

Jack shined the flashlight on the cover of the book. It showed huge trees partly hidden by mist. The title was:

AN AFRICAN RAIN FOREST

"*Rain* forest?" said Jack. "Good thing we brought our umbrella and flashlight. Remember the rain in the *Amazon* rain forest? Remember how dark it was under the treetops?"

"Yeah," said Annie. "Remember the spiders and scary ants?"

"Well . . . ," Jack said, "not all rain forests have the same bugs."

"Remember the river snakes?" said Annie. "And the crocodiles?"

7

"Well . . . ," said Jack, "not all rain forests have big rivers. There are different kinds of rain forests, you know."

"Right," said Annie. She pointed to the cover of the book. "I wish we could go there."

The wind started to blow.

"Oh, remember the jaguar?" said Annie. "And the vampire bats?"

"Wait!" said Jack.

But it was too late. The wind was blowing harder. The tree house started to spin.

It spun faster and faster.

Then everything was still.

Absolutely still.

# 2

## Cloud Forest

Jack opened his eyes.

"I can't tell *what* kind of rain forest this is," said Annie. She stared out the window.

Jack looked out, too. It seemed to be daytime, but he couldn't see much of anything. The quiet forest was covered with fog.

Jack opened their research book and read:

> **The misty rain forest in the mountains of central Africa is called a "cloud forest."**

"Oh, I get it," said Annie. "We're up so high, it's like we're in a cloud."

"Cool," said Jack. He pulled out his notebook and wrote:

cloud forest—rain forest high

up in mountains

Then he read more:

**The African cloud forest is home to
many animals, including elephants,
water buffaloes, black leopards . . .**

Jack looked up.

"Black leopards?" he said.

11

"Don't worry," said Annie.

Jack cleared his throat and kept reading:

**. . . antelopes, wild hogs, and gorillas.**

"*Gorillas?*" said Annie.

"Don't worry," said Jack.

"I'm not worried. I *love* gorillas," said Annie. "They're totally great!"

"I don't know about that," said Jack. He pictured huge apes pounding their chests. "I'd like to study them, though. Write down their habits and behavior, just like a real scientist."

"Whatever," said Annie. "Let's just go. This'll be a fun adventure!" She took off down the ladder.

Jack threw his notebook, the research book, and the flashlight into his pack. He hooked the umbrella over his arm. Then he followed Annie.

When they stepped onto the ground, Jack could see better. The fog had turned into a fine mist.

Jack and Annie started through the cloud forest. They walked around huge trees draped with moss. They pushed past tall shrubs and leafy plants.

"Wow, look at *that* tree," said Annie.

She pointed to a fat tree. It had wide lower limbs padded with thick cushions of moss.

"It looks like a piece of furniture," said Annie, "like an armchair."

"Yeah," said Jack. "I better draw it."

He put the umbrella on the ground. He pulled the flashlight out of his pack and put it next to the umbrella. Then he took out his notebook and pencil.

As Annie walked ahead, Jack started to draw a simple picture of the fat tree.

"Hey, Jack," Annie called in a whispery voice. "Come here. Quick!"

Jack grabbed his pack. He moved around the tree and caught up with Annie.

"Listen," she said.

Jack heard branches snap.

*Crack!*

*A leopard?* he wondered.

*Crack! Crack!*

Jack nervously looked around the forest.

"Maybe we should go back up to the tree house," he said. "We could read a little more and learn a little more."

Annie didn't answer. Jack turned to her.

She was grinning from ear to ear as she stared into the bushes. Jack followed her gaze.

A dark, shaggy little head was peeking out from a cluster of leaves.

"*Bu, bu?*" a small gorilla asked.

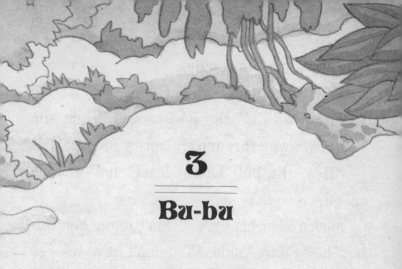

# 3

## Bu-bu

The gorilla's fur was very black against the green leaves. She had large nostrils and small ears. Her bright brown eyes were full of mischief.

"*Bu, bu, bu,*" she said. "*Bu, bu.*"

"*Bu, bu* yourself," said Annie.

The gorilla hid behind the leaves again. Then she poked her head out.

"Peekaboo!" said Annie.

The gorilla clapped her hands together.

She stuck out her tongue.

Jack and Annie both laughed.

*"Bu, bu, bu!"* the gorilla said. Then she bounded away through the misty forest.

"Hey, Bu-bu! Don't leave us!" Annie called.

Jack rolled his eyes. "Don't name her Bu-bu," he said to Annie. "You don't have to—"

"Wait, Bu-bu!" Annie shouted. She took off after the small gorilla.

"—turn every animal into your best friend," Jack finished. He shook his head. Then he made a list in his notebook.

gorilla behavior

plays peekaboo

claps hands

sticks out tongue

As he wrote, Jack heard Annie laughing. But then he heard high shrieks.

He caught his breath. *A leopard?* he wondered.

Carrying his notebook, Jack hurried in the direction of the noise. He found Annie and the small gorilla perched in two trees.

"What's wrong?" said Jack, standing beneath the trees.

"Nothing!" called Annie. "We're just playing."

The small gorilla screeched again. Then she scratched her head and hiccuped.

Annie screeched, too. She scratched *her* head and hiccuped.

While they played, Jack studied the gorilla a bit more.

He noticed she was about the size of a

19

three-year-old kid. Her fingers looked like human fingers. They even had fingernails! He made a new list:

<u>young gorilla</u>
size of 3-year-old
fingers like humans'
fingernails

Jack heard the tree leaves shaking. He looked up. Annie and the gorilla had both climbed higher.

"Hey, come down, Annie!" Jack called. "You might fall. Plus, it's getting dark."

Jack looked around. Light was fading quickly from the forest. *Is night falling?* he wondered. *Or is a storm coming?*

The small gorilla screeched again and climbed even higher.

"Hey, Bu-bu! Where you going?" said Annie. She climbed even higher, too.

"That's enough, Annie. Come down *now*!" said Jack. "I'm serious."

To his relief, the gorilla settled on a branch. Annie did the same.

The gorilla broke off a piece of tree bark. She nibbled it like a candy bar.

Annie broke off a piece of bark. She nibbled it like a candy bar, too.

The gorilla threw down her bark. She grabbed a tree branch and swung to another tree.

"Don't try it, Annie!" shouted Jack.

But his warning came too late.

Annie threw down her bark. She grabbed a tree branch and *tried* to swing to another tree.

Annie didn't swing like a gorilla. She fell

from the tree—and crashed down to the
ground near Jack.

"Annie!" he cried.

# 4

## Nightmare

Jack knelt beside Annie. She was gasping for breath.

The gorilla bounded down the tree and over to Annie. She bit her lower lip as if she were worried.

"Are you okay?" Jack asked Annie.

"Yes—" Annie panted, "just—got the breath—knocked out of me—"

"Wiggle your arms and your legs," said Jack.

Annie wiggled her arms and her legs.

"Good, nothing's broken," said Jack.

Just then, he felt a drop of water hit his arm. The mist had turned to rain.

"Uh-oh," said Jack. He threw his notebook into his pack.

"I better get our umbrella and flashlight," he said. "I left them near that tree that looked like a chair."

"I'll come, too," said Annie. She started to sit up.

"No, no, catch your breath," said Jack. "It's not far. I'll be right back."

He took off his jacket and draped it over her. "This'll help you stay dry," he said. He pulled on his pack and stood up.

The gorilla screeched.

"Stay with Annie!" said Jack.

Then he dashed back through the cloud forest. He looked for the fat tree with the wide limbs padded with moss.

As he peered through the growing darkness, Jack saw *many* fat trees. He saw *many* limbs padded with moss.

Soon he could hardly see trees at all. He realized that both a storm *and* night had come to the forest.

*Forget the umbrella and flashlight,* he thought. It was more important to get back to Annie before it was too dark. They could wait together for daylight.

As Jack started back to Annie, he could hardly see. He didn't know which way to go.

"Annie! Bu-bu!" he shouted. He felt silly shouting, "Bu-bu." But he didn't know what else to call the small gorilla.

Jack put out his hands. He moved slowly through the dark, rainy forest. He kept calling for Annie and Bu-bu. He listened for them. But he couldn't hear anything above the loud patter of the rain.

"Ahh!" he shouted. He had run into something that felt like a ball of spiderwebs!

As he jumped back, he slipped and fell in the mud. He crawled over to a tree and huddled between two of its giant roots.

*I'll just wait here until morning,* he thought. *Then I'll find Annie. Or she'll find me.*

As rain dripped all around him, Jack wondered if leopards came out at night. He quickly pushed the thought away. He tried to think about morning and finding Annie and going home.

He was *really* ready to go home.

*Why did Morgan even send us to the cloud forest?* he wondered. He tried to remember the secret rhyme.

*"To find a special magic . . . ,"* he whispered. He couldn't remember the rest. He felt tired and miserable. He took his backpack off and rested his head on it. He closed his eyes.

*"To find a special magic . . . ,"* he mumbled.

But he couldn't find the magic. He couldn't even find the words that finished the rhyme. Worst of all, he couldn't find Annie.

Their fun adventure in the cloud forest had turned into a nightmare.

# 5

## Silverback

Jack felt something tugging on his sleeve. He opened his eyes.

*Bu-bu.* The small gorilla was staring at him in the dawn light.

Jack stood up. His arms and legs felt stiff and achy. His wet clothes stuck to his skin.

He looked around the cloud forest. Misty sunlight shined through the tree branches.

"Where's Annie?" he asked the small gorilla.

Bu-bu waved her arms. Then she bounded off between the trees. Jack pulled on his pack and followed.

As the small gorilla led him through the cloud forest, her head bobbed above the leafy plants. Finally, she stopped before a row of shrubs.

Jack took a few steps forward and peered over the shrubs.

"Oh, man," he whispered.

Large dark figures were sleeping in an open, grassy area—*gorillas!* There were at least ten of them. Some slept on their backs. Some slept on their bellies.

The gorillas were all sizes. The smallest was a baby sleeping in its mother's arms. The biggest was a giant with black and silver fur.

Jack pulled the book out of his pack. He

found a chapter on gorillas and read:

> Mountain gorillas live together in
> families. The leader of the family is
> a large male called a "silverback"
> because he has silver fur on his back
> and shoulders. Gorillas do not hunt
> other animals. They mainly eat the
> plant growth of the forest. They are
> known to be shy and gentle giants.

"*Shy and gentle giants*," Jack repeated. That sounded good.

He peered over the shrubs again. Bu-bu waved at him. She was standing at the far edge of the clearing. She pointed to something in the tall grass.

Annie was fast asleep in the grass!

Jack didn't know what to do. If he called her name, the gorillas would wake up. He had only one choice. He had to sneak over to her.

Jack put his book in his pack. He pushed past the shrubs and stepped into the clearing. His heart was pounding. He thought of the words from the book—*shy and gentle giants.*

As he started toward Annie, he heard a grunt. The giant gorilla with silver fur opened his eyes. When the gorilla saw Jack, he sat up.

Jack stopped in his tracks.

The gorilla just glared. *This* giant did not seem shy or gentle at all.

Jack saw a stick lying on the ground. He picked it up—just in case.

Jack's stick made the gorilla growl. He stood up. He was *very* tall and *very* wide.

Jack dropped his stick.

Bu-bu ran and hid behind a tree.

The silverback growled again. His long, shaggy arms touched the ground. His fingers curled under. Walking on his knuckles, he stepped toward Jack.

Jack stepped back.

The gorilla stepped forward.

Jack stepped back again.

The gorilla kept stepping forward. Jack kept stepping back until he had stepped out of the clearing.

But the silverback kept coming. Jack stumbled back through the brush until he came to a thick wall of plants.

The gorilla kept coming. Jack couldn't move back anymore.

"Uh . . . hi," he said nervously. He held up his hand. "I come in—"

Before Jack could say "peace," the giant gorilla went crazy. He hooted and leaped to his feet.

Jack crouched down in a panic.

The gorilla kept hooting. He grabbed a tree limb. He shook it wildly. He ripped leaves from branches.

He gnashed his teeth. He cupped his hands. He beat his chest.

*WRAAGH!* he roared. *WRAAGH!*

The gorilla dropped on all fours. He charged back and forth past Jack. Then he threw himself on his belly. He began bashing the ground with his palms. He bashed and bashed and bashed.

Jack scrambled on his hands and knees over to a tree. He hid behind the trunk, hugging his head.

He waited for the maniac gorilla to find him and tear him to pieces.

# 6

## Good Morning, Gorillas

The pounding ended. There was silence . . . a long silence.

Jack opened his eyes. He peeked around the tree. The silverback was sitting on the ground. His lips were curved in a smile. He looked pleased with himself.

*Was his whole act a fake?* Jack wondered.

Jack didn't know whether to be scared or to laugh. The only thing he *did* know was he still had to get to Annie!

Jack pulled out the research book. He found the gorilla chapter again. He read:

> To safely get close to gorillas in the wild, it's wise to act like a gorilla yourself. Crouch down and rest on your knuckles like a gorilla. Keep your head down and act friendly!

Jack packed up his research book. He put his pack on his back. Then he went down on his knees.

Jack took a deep breath. He smiled a friendly smile. Pressing down on his knuckles, he moved out from behind the tree. His fingers hurt as he walked on them.

The silverback grunted.

Jack didn't look up. He kept smiling a friendly smile as he crawled through the brush toward the clearing.

When he got to the edge of the clearing, he glanced back. The giant gorilla was following him. He was frowning, but he didn't seem about to attack.

Jack kept going. He moved into the clearing. Then he stopped.

More gorillas were waking up. A large gorilla hugged Bu-bu as if to comfort her.

When Bu-bu saw Jack, she screeched joyfully.

All the other gorillas turned to look at him. They made nervous sounds.

Jack's heart pounded. But he just smiled his friendly smile and kept crawling. He crawled around the gorillas and over to Annie.

"Wake up!" he said, shaking her.

Annie yawned, then opened her eyes.

"Oh, hi!" she said.

"Are you okay?" asked Jack.

"Sure," she said. She sat up and looked around. She gasped.

The gorillas were staring at Jack and Annie with bright, darting eyes. The silver-back stared the hardest.

"Oh, wow!" said Annie. A joyful smile crossed her face. "Good morning, gorillas!"

# 7

## Eating Out

Annie kept smiling at the gorillas. "Wow!" she said. "Wow, wow, wow."

"Didn't you know you were sleeping next to them?" Jack asked.

"No!" she said. "When you didn't come back, Bu-bu led me here. But I couldn't see anything. It was too dark."

Just then, Bu-bu left her mother's arms and bounded over to Annie. She climbed into Annie's lap and hugged her.

Another small gorilla left his mother and ran over to Annie, too. He was about the size of a two-year-old kid.

"*Ho, ho!*" he said. He gave Annie a playful poke.

"Ho, ho yourself!" said Annie. "Is Ho-ho your name?"

She tickled Ho-ho. She tickled Bu-bu, too. The two small gorillas made laughing sounds and fell onto their backs.

The two mother gorillas laughed, too. *Huh-huh-huh*, they said.

Jack felt a little jealous. He wanted the gorillas to like him as well. But he didn't know how to join in the fun. So he just sighed and pulled out his notebook. He added to his "gorilla behavior" list:

gorillas like to tickle and laugh

Suddenly, he heard a low growl.

He looked up. The silverback had moved closer to him. He was glaring.

"That big guy doesn't understand what you're doing!" Annie called to Jack. "He's never seen anyone take notes before."

Jack quickly put his notebook away.

The giant gorilla huffed. Then he turned to his family and gave a short bark.

The gorillas began lining up behind the silverback. The baby traveled in his mother's arms. Ho-ho traveled on his mother's back. Bu-bu and Annie held hands. They all followed the silverback out of the clearing.

"Come on!" Annie called to Jack. "Let's go with Big Guy and the gang!"

Jack shook his head.

"I don't think they want *me* to come along," he said.

Bu-bu screeched at Jack. She held out her free hand to him.

"*Bu-bu* wants you!" said Annie.

Jack smiled shyly. He took Bu-bu's small, warm hand. Then he walked with Annie and the gorillas out of the clearing.

On their ramble through the cloud forest, the gorillas found food everywhere. They munched flowers and ferns and leaves. They swallowed and burped.

They munched twigs and branches and pieces of bark and bamboo. They swallowed and burped.

As the gorillas ate breakfast, it started to rain again. But they didn't seem to mind.

Annie didn't seem to mind, either. She and Bu-bu played tag in the drizzly woods. They ran around the trees, laughing and screeching.

Jack tried to follow them, but he gave up. He was tired and cold. Shivering, he stood under a mossy tree to keep dry.

While he was alone, Jack sneaked his notebook out of his pack. He made a new list:

gorilla foods

flowers

ferns

leaves

twigs

bark

branches

bamboo

As he wrote, he heard a low growl. He looked up.

Big Guy had spotted him. The silverback

was standing close by. He was frowning at Jack, his lips tucked in a tight line.

"Sorry, sorry!" said Jack. He quickly put away his notebook.

Big Guy kept frowning.

Jack quickly tried to act like a gorilla. He went down on all fours. He tore off the leaf of a plant. He took a bite. It tasted bitter, like vinegar. Jack pretended to munch and swallow and burp.

Big Guy huffed, then moved on. As soon as he was gone, Jack spat out the leaf.

"Yuck, yuck, yuck!" he said, wiping his tongue.

Jack felt a tap on his back. He jumped. But it was just Ho-ho. The small gorilla offered him a twig to eat.

"Oh, no thanks, Ho-ho," said Jack.

Ho-ho kept holding out the twig.

"Oh, okay," said Jack, politely taking it. "I'll eat it later." He put the twig into his backpack.

Ho-ho's mom came over to Jack. She held some berries to his lips.

"Uh, no thanks," Jack said.

The gorilla stared at him with a sad look.

"Oh, okay," said Jack. He opened his mouth. And Ho-ho's mom fed him the berries.

Jack munched the berries. To his surprise, they tasted good. He swallowed, then burped just like a gorilla. This time, he wasn't pretending.

Bu-bu's mom then came over to Jack. She offered him some rainwater from a cupped plant. Jack was very thirsty. He sipped the water. It tasted fresh and cold.

Bu-bu's mom took Jack's hand in her wide hand. She led him through the forest to Annie and Bu-bu.

Bu-bu screeched happily when she saw Jack. She threw her furry arms around him.

"Hi! We missed you!" Annie said to Jack. "Are you having fun?"

Jack smiled and nodded.

Actually, he *was* having fun now. He didn't mind the rain so much anymore. He didn't feel so left out. Some of the gorillas really seemed to like him, he thought. They seemed to like him a lot.

# 8

## A Special Language

The rain ended. Slowly the feeding came to a stop.

Big Guy led his family into a clearing. The tall grass sparkled with misty sunlight.

The silverback lay down and tucked his arms under his head.

The other gorillas gathered around him. Some beat the grasses until they were flat.

Ho-ho's mom made a bed of weed stalks for Ho-ho. Bu-bu's mom made a bed of leaves for Bu-bu. Then she made two extra beds for Jack and Annie.

They lay down with all the gorillas to take their naps. Jack used his backpack for a pillow.

Lying on his leafy bed, Jack watched the mother of the baby gorilla groom her small baby. The mother parted his hair and searched through it, picking at his skin now and then.

The baby soon wiggled free and crawled around in the grass. His mother's gaze then rested on Annie. She moved over to Annie and gently grabbed one of her pigtails. She studied it carefully.

"What are you doing?" Annie asked.

"She's looking for bugs, I think," said Jack.

"Oh, yuck!" said Annie, sitting up.

Jack laughed. Just then, the baby's mother reached for him.

"Oops! No thanks! No bugs on me!" he said, and he sat up, too.

The mother gorilla lay back in the grass and closed her eyes. Her baby crawled over to Annie.

"Hi, Little Guy," Annie said tenderly. She picked up the baby and stroked his head. The baby smiled at her and closed his eyes.

While all the gorillas napped, Jack sneaked the book out of his pack. He found the gorilla chapter. He read softly to Annie:

> Gorillas are very smart. A captive gorilla named Koko has even learned sign language. Sign language is a special language used by people who cannot hear. Koko can say—

"*What?*" Annie said loudly. "*Sign* language? A *special language*?"

Her voice woke Bu-bu and Ho-ho. They sat up and rubbed their eyes.

"So?" said Jack.

"Morgan's secret *rhyme*!" said Annie. "Don't you remember?" She repeated the rhyme:

> *To find a special kind of magic*
> *in worlds so far apart,*
> *speak a special language,*
> *talk with your hands and heart.*

"Oh . . . yeah!" said Jack.

"I even know a little sign language," said Annie. "In school, we learned how to sign *I love you.*"

Annie held up a closed hand. Slowly she lifted her thumb, index finger, and little finger. She showed the sign to Bu-bu and Ho-ho.

"I—love—you," she said slowly.

The small gorillas looked curious.

Jack made the sign, too.

"I—love—you," he said to Bu-bu and Ho-ho.

The two little gorillas stared at Annie and Jack. Then both of them held up their hands. They tried to make the same sign.

"They love us, too!" said Annie.

"Wow," said Jack. He glanced over at Big Guy.

The silverback's eyes were open! He was watching them. Jack quickly closed the book. To his relief, the giant gorilla turned over.

"Well," Annie said with a sigh, "I guess that does it."

"We spoke a special language," said Jack. "We talked with our—" Before he could finish his sentence, Bu-bu pushed him.

"Whoa!" said Jack.

Ho-ho held his little arms above his head. He reared back and charged at Jack. With a flying tackle, he knocked Jack over.

"What's going on?" said Jack.

"They want to play with you!" said Annie.

Bu-bu jumped on Jack and put him in a headlock. Jack broke free from the two small gorillas. He jumped up and dashed into the forest.

Bu-bu and Ho-ho charged after him.

Annie carried Little Guy and followed. She laughed as the small gorillas looked for Jack.

Jack hid behind a tree. He pushed his glasses into place. He waited for Bu-bu.

In a moment, she walked by.

"BOO!" Jack shouted, jumping out.

Bu-bu screeched and leaped straight up in the air. Jack cracked up laughing.

Bu-bu didn't laugh, though. She bit her lip. She hid her face behind her hands.

"Ohhh, Bu-bu," said Annie. "Don't be scared."

She gently put the baby on the ground. She reached out to comfort Bu-bu.

Bu-bu wrapped her arms around Annie's

neck. She buried her furry head in Annie's shoulder.

"Jack was just playing," said Annie.

Bu-bu raised her head. She looked at Jack over Annie's shoulder.

"Friends?" he asked softly.

Bu-bu stuck her tongue out at him.

Jack laughed. Bu-bu showed her teeth in a big smile.

"Friends!" said Jack.

Just then, Ho-ho started screeching. Jack and Annie looked around. Ho-ho was pointing into the bushes.

"Where's Little Guy?" said Annie. She and Jack dashed around the shrubs.

The baby had crawled to a tree. He was looking up at a branch.

A huge, sleek cat with black fur was sitting on the branch. His pale green eyes stared down at the baby gorilla. He looked hungry.

"*A black leopard,*" breathed Jack.

The leopard leaped lightly down from his perch. He faced Little Guy. The baby looked scared.

"No!" cried Annie.

She ran over to the baby gorilla and scooped him into her arms.

The leopard let out a snarl. He lowered his head and started slowly toward Annie and the baby.

Jack panicked. He didn't know what to do at first. Then he remembered Big Guy's act. Jack took a deep breath. When he let it out, he made a loud hooting sound.

He tore out from the brush. Hooting like a silverback, he ran between Annie and the leopard.

Jack grabbed a tree limb and shook it. He ripped leaves from branches.

He cupped his hands. He beat his chest.

*"WRAAGH!"* he roared. *"WRAAGH!"*

Then Jack leaned over and charged back and forth past the leopard.

Finally, he threw himself on his belly. He began bashing the ground with his palms. He bashed and bashed and bashed.

"Jack!" Annie called. "Jack!"

Jack looked up.

"He's gone," Annie said in a quiet voice. "The leopard's gone. He left a while ago."

"Oh," said Jack.

He sat up.

He pushed his glasses into place. He looked around. Then he smiled.

# 9

## Good-bye, Gorillas

Jack couldn't stop smiling. He had scared off a leopard!

Bu-bu and Ho-ho stared at Jack with awe. Annie looked at him with awe, too.

"When did you learn to do *that*?" she asked.

Before Jack could answer, he heard a rustling in the brush. Then Big Guy stepped out from the shrubs.

The giant gorilla walked silently over to Annie. He took Little Guy from her and put the baby on his back. Then he touched Annie's cheek gently.

Annie grinned at him.

Bu-bu and Ho-ho ran to Big Guy and clung to his legs.

The giant gorilla barked at the small ones, directing them to come with him.

As he walked past Jack, Big Guy stopped.

*Huh-huh-huh,* he said in a low voice. He reached out toward Jack.

Jack ducked.

But the silverback patted him on the head. Then he and the small gorillas moved out of sight.

Jack felt as if the top of his head were glowing.

"Wow," he whispered. "Did you see what he just did?"

"Yeah," said Annie. "He must have

watched the show you put on. He was proud of you."

"Well, he was proud of you, too," Jack said modestly.

Annie nodded, smiling. "I guess it's time to leave now," she said.

"Leave?" said Jack.

"We have to say good-bye now," said Annie.

"Good-bye?" said Jack. He didn't want to say good-bye to the gorillas. He loved them. They were totally great.

"Yeah," Annie said softly. "Come on."

She led the way back through the shrubs, around the trees, to the clearing.

They found all the gorillas awake. Some were stretching and yawning. Others were munching on grass or leaves.

The baby was back in his mother's arms. Bu-bu and Ho-ho were chattering away to their moms.

*They're probably telling them what I did,* Jack thought.

He and Annie walked over to Big Guy and stood in front of him. The other gorillas gathered around.

"We have to go now," Annie said to all of them.

"We have to say good-bye," said Jack.

"Thanks for letting us be a part of your family," said Annie.

She and Jack held up their hands and waved. The gorillas looked sad. They murmured soft sounds.

Big Guy lifted his hand in the air as if he were about to wave. But instead, the silverback raised his thumb, his index finger, and his little finger.

*I love you*, the giant gorilla signed.

Jack couldn't believe his eyes.

Annie signed back, *I love you.*

Jack signed, too.

The silverback stared at them for a long moment with a gentle, shy look. Then he turned away and gave a short bark to his family.

All the gorillas lined up behind him. The baby's mother held her baby close. Ho-ho rode piggyback on his mom. Bu-bu held her mom's hand.

The silverback started away from the clearing. The others followed.

Bu-bu was the only one who looked back. She screeched and waved at Jack and Annie. Then she walked away, out of sight.

Jack couldn't talk. His heart was too full. He took a few steps in the direction of the gorillas.

"Hey—" Annie said softly. "You're going the wrong way."

Jack looked back at her.

"The tree house is over there," she said. She pointed in the opposite direction—at the tree house peeking out from the fog.

Jack sighed. Then he turned and started to follow her out of the clearing.

"Oh, don't forget this," said Annie.

She leaned over and picked up Jack's backpack from the grass. She handed it to him.

"Thanks," he said.

They kept walking.

"And don't forget *this*," said Annie. She picked up Jack's jacket from under a tree. She handed it to him.

"Thanks," said Jack. He tied his jacket around his waist. They kept walking.

"And don't forget *these*," said Annie. She pointed to the flashlight and umbrella. They lay on the grass under the wide, mossy limbs of a fat tree.

Annie picked them up and carried them herself.

It started to drizzle again just as she and Jack got to the rope ladder. They climbed up into the tree house.

When they got inside, they looked out the window. Jack hoped to catch one last glimpse of the gorilla family.

But there was nothing to see. A white mist covered the cloud forest.

Annie picked up the Pennsylvania book. She pointed to a picture of Frog Creek woods.

"I wish we could go home," she said.

Suddenly, a joyous screech rang out. The

happy, wild sound shot through the white mist, through the cool rain, straight into Jack's heart.

He opened his mouth to answer the call of the gorillas. But it was too late. The wind began to blow.

The tree house started to spin.

It spun faster and faster.

Then everything was still.

Absolutely still.

# 10

## A Special Magic

*Tap-tap-tap.*

Jack opened his eyes.

The Frog Creek woods were still dark and rainy.

"We're home," Annie said.

Jack sighed.

"I miss them already," he said.

"Me too," said Annie. "Did you take a lot of notes on their habits and behavior?"

Jack shrugged.

"I listed a few things about them," he said. "But sometimes lists don't tell you much. You have to love gorillas to *really* know them."

"Yeah. That's right," said Annie.

Jack opened his backpack. He pulled out their research book and put it in the corner.

Then he pulled out the twig that Ho-ho had given him. He smiled as he showed it to Annie.

"I promised Ho-ho I'd eat this later," he said. "But I think we should save it for Morgan instead."

"Good idea," said Annie. "It'll prove to her that we found a special magic."

"Yeah, *gorilla* magic," said Jack.

"The magic of *all* animals," said Annie.

"Yeah," said Jack.

He placed the twig next to the scrolls they'd brought back from old England.

"Let's go," said Annie. She started down.

Jack pulled on his backpack. He put the flashlight in his pack. Then he grabbed the umbrella and followed Annie.

They started through the Frog Creek woods. It was still cool and dark and rainy.

Jack didn't mind, though. He didn't put on his jacket. He didn't take out the flashlight. He didn't put up the umbrella.

Jack felt as if he weren't completely human yet. There was still a bit of gorilla left in him.

"*Ho, ho, ho,*" he said in a low voice.

"*Bu, bu,*" Annie said back.

"*Huh, huh, huh,*" they said together.

# MORE FACTS FOR
## JACK AND ANNIE AND *YOU*!

Gorillas are the biggest members of the group of animals we call *primates*. Other primates include chimpanzees, orangutans, gibbons, baboons, monkeys, and humans.

All gorillas live in Africa. There are three groups of gorillas—western lowland gorillas, eastern lowland gorillas, and mountain gorillas. Mountain gorillas are the largest gorillas. They have longer hair and longer jaws and teeth than lowland gorillas.

Mountain gorillas live in the volcanic mountains of Virunga in east-central Africa. The word *virunga* means "a lonely mountain that reaches to the clouds."

Gorillas are mainly *herbivores*, or plant-eaters. They keep on the move, so they will not deplete a feeding area. A silverback gorilla can eat up to 50 pounds of forest vegetation in only one day.

# ENDANGERED SPECIES

All gorillas are on the endangered species list. But the ones most threatened are the mountain gorillas. Fewer than 650 still live in the wild. None live in captivity. A woman named Dian Fossey lived for almost 20 years with the mountain gorillas. During her life, she fought very hard for their protection.

# GORILLAS AND
# AMERICAN SIGN LANGUAGE

Since 1971, a lowland gorilla named Koko has been part of a gorilla language project in California. Gorillas will never be able to talk like people because their vocal cords cannot make the necessary range of sounds. But a woman named Penny Patterson taught Koko the gorilla how to use *American Sign Language*. American Sign Language is a special language using hand gestures. It is primarily used by people who are unable to hear. Koko has learned to make more than 1,000 signs. And she understands about 2,000 English words. She proves that gorillas have extraordinary intelligence, as well as many thoughts and feelings similar to those of humans.

Don't miss the next Magic Tree House book,
when Jack and Annie meet the Pilgrims and
cause trouble at dinner in . . .

# MAGIC TREE HOUSE® #27

## THANKSGIVING ON THURSDAY

**Will Jack and Annie solve
all of Morgan le Fay's riddles?
Can they find the special kinds of magic?
What other adventures will they have?
Read and find out!**

# Want to learn more about rain forests?

*Get the facts behind the fiction in the Magic Tree House® Research Guide.*

Available now!

# Discover the facts
## behind the fiction with the

# MAGIC TREE HOUSE®
## RESEARCH GUIDES

The must-have, all-true companions for your favorite Magic Tree House® adventures!

# Around the World with Jack and Annie!

You have traveled to far away places and have been
on countless Magic Tree House adventures.
Now is your chance to receive an official
Magic Tree House passport and collect official stamps
for each destination from around the world!

## HOW

## Get your exclusive Magic Tree House Passport!*

Send your name, street address, city, state, zip code, and date of birth to:
The Magic Tree House Passport, Random House Children's Books,
Marketing Department, 1745 Broadway, 10th Floor, New York, NY 10019

OR log on to **www.magictreehouse.com/passport**
to download and print your passport now!

## Collect Official Magic Tree House Stamps:

Log on to **www.magictreehouse.com** to submit your answer to the
trivia questions below. If you answer correctly, you will automatically
receive your official stamp for Book 26: *Good Morning, Gorillas.*

1. What does Annie call the first small gorilla she meets?

2. What animal does Jack scare off?

3. What does Ho-ho's mom give Jack to eat?

# Guess what?
## *Jack and Annie have a musical CD!*

For more information about
MAGIC TREE HOUSE: THE MUSICAL
(including how to order the CD!),
visit www.mthmusical.com.

# SILENT NIGHT

# WILL MOSES

# SILENT NIGHT

PUFFIN BOOKS

# SILENT NIGHT

Once on a silent night in a place where snow clouds clung to the Vermont hills and lay heavily over every farmhouse and barn, over shops and country lanes, everyone was getting ready.

Benjamin Rogers, proprietor of the general store, was refilling his flour

barrels and stocking shelves. The carolers, including Teasy Simpson and little Ephraim Simpson, were gathering up their warmest scarves and toboggans, preparing to meet in the center of the town commons later that evening. Deacon Henry Heinz, from down by Parsons Creek, was already lighting the church lamps.

And up the valley somewhere beyond the Millers' farm, where the

headwaters of the Black Creek rise, Tom Henry and his little brother, Andy, were skating home with the evergreen they'd just cut in tow. On an ordinary day those two boys would frolic for hours on the ice, skating whirls and twirls, having the grandest time cutting fancy sixes and eights.

Today, though, was no ordinary day. The tree they were pulling was more gangly and unruly than they'd ever imagined when earlier they'd spied it growing in the nearby woods. And both boys knew this day might have more surprises left in it. So with all their might, they made a straight dash for home.

Tom Henry and Andy had to get ready, too.

# HOLY NIGHT

Now look at that sky," James Miller called when he saw his boys coming across the field. "Beautiful. Just beautiful." He marched his milk cows right through a flock of hens that had been contentedly pecking about the farmyard, and off they shot, flapping and cackling like they'd been insulted. "It's a holy-night sky, boys. You'll want to remember this night."

It was indeed a beautiful early-evening sky, with brilliant splinters of fading pink sunlight still mingling wildly with blue and gray storm clouds on the distant horizon. "Oh, come on, boys, come on, then," James Miller said as the last cow was herded into the barn. "Let's see if we can't get to the station and back home again before the weather becomes unfit for man or beast. There's a train we've got to meet."

The boys knew Pa was talking about the 5:15 local from Bellows Falls.

"To pick up Grandma Stokes, Pa?" Tom Henry called out. "Well, Tom Henry," Pa called back, "don't she come every year, like clockwork?" He liked Grandma Stokes—General Grant, he called her when she was out of earshot.

Tom Henry and Andy finished up their chores—collecting eggs from the henhouse—all the while thinking how Pa had a lot more on his mind tonight than a snowstorm or the arrival of Grandma Stokes.

From the horse barn, Pa led old Peg and Mary, his favorite team, and hitched them to the sleigh. Tom Henry ran the basket of fresh eggs up to the house, fetched the warming stones for the sleigh, and he hung up his skates in the woodshed. Andy threw his skates over his shoulder and helped Pa with the team, for in the winter months, wherever Andy went, his skates went, too. Even to the train station.

## ALL IS CALM

Then they all climbed into the sleigh and pulled up the buffalo robe. As they drove by the house, Pa took a last long look through the window of the room where Mama was. Then he barked, "Giddy-yap, Peg. Giddy-yap, Mary," and *whissh,* away they went, trotting down the snowy lane.

Andy knew Pa didn't want to leave home at all tonight. Not now, anyway.

Like a sheetful of cotton thrown to the wind, the snowflakes started falling before Peg and Mary had taken the sleigh a half mile down the lane. Past the sycamore and maple and oak trees, and between the stone walls that lined the old roadway, they trotted on. Through the covered bridge, the horses' hooves clopped over the rattly boards.

And then the sleigh glided out: it was suddenly quiet, like coming out of a dark, echoing cave into a white, feathery world again. Even the dull beat of the horses' hooves seemed distant now.

Andy pulled the buffalo robe up tighter. Usually when they made this trip, Pa would stop the sleigh and let him out just so he could skate the frozen river. He'd race down the icy stream, trying with all his might to beat Pa and his sleigh to Butternut Bend, where the river and road went their separate ways. Most times Andy would win. How that boy loved to skate.

Tonight, though, wasn't usually. Tonight, he just listened to the quiet of that snowy valley, a special quiet that seemed to surround them all.

"It won't be long now, boys," Pa said as the sleigh drove into town. Andy knew Pa was talking about more than catching the 5:15 train.

# ALL IS BRIGHT

The little village was all astir as the townsfolk scurried about, doing last-minute errands. Light glowed from lantern upon lantern, and the windows twinkled, giving the shops and houses a magical appearance.

"Are you ready up at your place, then, James?" Fred, the blacksmith, called out as the sleigh passed. Fred was twisting up a fancy metal ornament in the brilliant orange fire of the forge —a special gift for his own dear wife.

Pa nodded and smiled through the feathery snow. "Yes, sir, Fred, nearly ready. Least my stocking is hung."

Fred just grinned and waved back.

As the sleigh went by the church, carolers began pouring out of the door, each bundled head to toe in woolens. And each with a lantern in one hand and a songbook in the other.

"My heavens, James, is this a time for you three boys to be out having a joyride for yourselves?" Teasy Simpson, the town's busybody, called out as she lit her own lantern.

"Meeting the five-fifteen," Pa called back. "Important visitor arriving, surprised you didn't know all about it."

Pa pulled the sleigh up to the general store, and went in just long enough to get some fresh coffee beans for General Grant—Pa knew Grandma liked her coffee strong and black. And while he was at it, he picked up some horehound candy from the barrel for himself and the boys. In case there was a wait at the station.

"A-yeh, James. Surprised to see you here today," Benjamin Rogers said, teasing Pa in his shopkeeper way. The other men, clustered around the potbellied stove just as they were every day, nodded. They, too, were prodding Pa to give up some gossip. Pa just popped a horehound candy into his mouth, smiled, and out of the store he walked.

Under way again, Andy could hear the distant moan of the train whistle as the team trotted past the town green, now white under its winter blanket. Past Foster's Wagon Shop, with its upper floor hanging over the road, back toward the river and Peterson's Grist Mill, its giant wheel still churning, over the bridge spanning the gorge with its gold-green water racing toward the Connecticut, Peg and Mary flew to meet the 5:15.

# ROUND YON VIRGIN

**I**t was Tinker, Mama's old quilty friend, who ran out of Mama's room and told Cozy, the milkmaid, who in turn ran to get Old Paul, the hired man,

who went down to the barn and rousted Josiah, the mule, out of his stall. He simply jumped on his bare back, and rode Josiah for all he was worth through that snowy night.

Surely Old Paul was worried about the weather, and he kept a wary eye on the cloud-puffed sky. Surely he was worried about James and the boys. But all said and done, Old Paul had bigger worries. Worries that drove him out into the stormy winter's night.

Old Paul was riding feverishly up Maiden Lane toward the big, crooked maple tree, when Doc Herrick saw him through his window. As wise as he was, Doc Herrick knew exactly why Old Paul was there. He gave a tender good-bye kiss to his sweet wife, Missy Herrick, and pulled on his boots, his overcoat, his hat,

and the striped muffler Missy had made for him that very December. Then, grabbing his bag, he gave the twins, Sophie and Olivia (who were not at all happy he was leaving), a hug and kiss, and he ran out to the barn.

Old Paul had already hitched Herrick's horse Jenny to the sleigh. Like a lightning bolt, the sleigh burst out of the barn doors into the deepening snow.

Luckily at the station the 5:15 was on time despite the storm, and naturally General Grant was the first off the train.

"There she is, just like I knew she would be," Pa said with a grin, and

with Grandma up front, they all climbed into the sleigh, squeezed tight among her satchels and sweet-smelling bundles. Doc Herrick and Old Paul, Pa and The General, Tom Henry and Andy were all going to the same place—the farm on Sycamore Lane.

"Do you think we will make it in time, James?" The General asked Pa. Her satchel nudged him in the ribs.

"We'll make it, Granny," Pa said. "It's Christmas Eve, isn't it?"

"I hope you're right," she said. A gust of icy wind stole her words. They all knew this would be a Christmas Eve like no other, and they went on into the dark, snowy night.

# MOTHER AND CHILD

Doc Herrick got to the old farmhouse on Sycamore Lane first, and in minutes the place came alive. Old Paul had already finished stabling Jenny and was just crossing the farmyard when Pa's sleigh pulled up.

"Is it time?" Pa shouted to Old Paul.

"No, sir," said Paul. "Things are just starting to happen."

And sure enough, wasn't Old Paul right? No sooner had he walked into the house carrying a giant armful of wood for the cookstove than General Grant began to issue orders.

"Doc Herrick needs hot water! Paul, pump some, quick. Get it on the stove to boil. And Tinker, don't be in a hurry to leave on such a night

as this. You can help—start by making strong coffee. Like as not, we will want plenty of it." Then Cozy, the milkmaid, came in from doing chores. "Cozy," Grandma said, "we're going to need a meal before this night is out. See what you can find to put on the table to feed all these hungry folks!"

Pa's eyes twinkled as he grinned. With General Grant in charge, things were certainly bound to happen. Pa and everyone else there hoped it would be soon.

The tall old clock in the parlor, the one Andy liked so much, with the little moon creeping across the face, struck nine and then ten and then eleven o'clock. Pa, Tom Henry, and Andy had just enough time to trim the tree.

They had nearly forgotten about it. Grandma remembered, though, and made sure they got it up and in just the right spot!

They trimmed every branch of that tree, stringing it with popcorn and strands of fragrant apple curls and cranberries. They hung tin icicles and ornaments from the boughs, along with wonderful old glass balls, candy canes, and even some tiny rag dolls.

Then they set the tree candles and Pa lifted Andy up high so he could place the old glass star, the one that had been Mama's when she was a little girl, atop the tree. It was a crookedy old tree, and maybe they hadn't trimmed it just the way Mama would have done, but it was pert and

sparkly. Particularly with the glass star on top reflecting the light of the room the way it did. It shone sweetly and cast wonderful star shadows across the room.

"It's a miracle," said Pa. Andy knew Pa was talking about more than that twinkling glass star.

It was now nearly midnight. *Bong, bong, bong* . . . went the clock. Its sleepy little moon moved across its face until the clock struck twelve.

Well, it wasn't more than a minute or two after the clock clapped twelve when a cry went up in Mama's bedroom. It was a new voice. A new cry. Andy suddenly felt his heart lurch.

# HOLY INFANT

Pa went in first with Tom Henry and little Andy. Didn't they creep in nice and quiet. Doc Herrick, certainly the wise one this night, was there, and so were Tinker and Cozy. Looking over everyone, of course, was The General. And there in bed, midst all these people, were Mama and a just-born, tiny little Christmas baby.

Somewhere out in the valley, carolers were singing. Maybe down at Sissy Atkins' or at the Jones Farm. Maybe they were singing their hearts out for the midnight service. Who knew? In that room, though, the only music heard—trumpets and angels' voices—came from some warm place inside each person, as everyone looked at Mama and her newborn baby for the first time.

"Now," whispered Pa, breaking the spell, "isn't that a holy child." Andy thought she was.

# SO TENDER AND MILD

**W**hat started the gift-giving is hard to figure, it being so late and all. Tinker took a quilt she'd made by hand—it had sailboats, bears, and rocking horses, and all sorts of fine stitching. "Just right for the new baby," she said,

and tucked it up under the little baby's chin. Old Paul brought out a hand-some, carved wooden horse. "Made from the old beech tree struck by light-nin' two years ago," he said with a smile. Cozy, not quite so handy with needle and thread, did in fact make a tiny little nightgown for the baby (out of a pretty old petticoat). With a blushing smile, she laid it out on the bed.

Granny rummaged around in one of her bundles and soon enough fished out a dandy little yellow knit sweater with a hand-crocheted lace collar. Right then she didn't seem so much like General Grant after all.

Then Tom Henry stepped up to that baby, who seemed no bigger than one of Pa's hands, and he gave her the jar with the old bees' nest in it—the one he found hanging in the attic last spring. In the dim twinkling light of that room, it looked like a jar of jewels. Ma smiled

at Tom Henry, then back at the baby, so tender, so mild.

Little Andy wished he had known people were going to be giving gifts.

# SLEEP IN HEAVENLY PEACE

Now the news went out over that snowy Vermont valley. Old Paul and Cozy saw to that. Down Sycamore Lane with its giant trees looking like white-haired, bearded kings. To the Atkins' farm, where the Atkins had just hung their stockings and gone to bed. Over to the Ketcham cottage, where they were trying their best not to open their gifts till morning. Just like the wintery north wind, the news of that night swept down the valley. Before long it even reached the carolers, who were just on their way home from singing at the midnight church service.

Well, didn't those wonderful, bone-tired carolers come trudging up Sycamore Lane when they heard the news? They formed up their choir right outside Mama's window, where that dear baby had just fallen asleep.

"Silent night, holy night," they sang, tenor voices rolling right into the dark. "Holy infant so tender and mild," they sang, the sopranos and altos harmonizing. "Sleep in heavenly peace," they sang all together. All those tired-but-loving voices, never sounding sweeter, sang out through the wintery night to that tiny little Christmas baby cradled in her mother's arms.

# SLEEP IN HEAVENLY PEACE

**S**urely, it was a miracle. But now it was time for everyone to get some rest, at least that's what The General said. The carolers went home pretty quick after their last song, for the night was growing colder. They all had icy frost hanging from scarves and mustaches.

Tinker left with them, arm in arm, huddling close to keep warm. Old Paul went to his room over the woodshed; the ride and excitement sure had tuckered him out. Cozy crawled into bed in the little room off the kitchen and pulled three quilts snug, right up to her nose.

Doc Herrick and Jenny drove on home through the snow, though he knew well enough that the twins and Missy were fast asleep in their beds. He had missed Christmas Eve with them, but being part of a Christmas miracle was pretty special, too. Each time Doc brought a babe into this world, it seemed a miracle to him.

Pa took the candle, and he and Tom Henry slowly climbed up the stairs, singing in a loud whisper as they went, "Hark! the her-ald an-gels sing, Glory to the newborn King!" Pa turned when he saw Andy wasn't with them. "Come on along to bed, Andy, it's late."

But Andy didn't come. Instead, he went back to Mama's bedroom. Mama was sound asleep, and so was the babe. He quietly tiptoed over to the old featherbed.

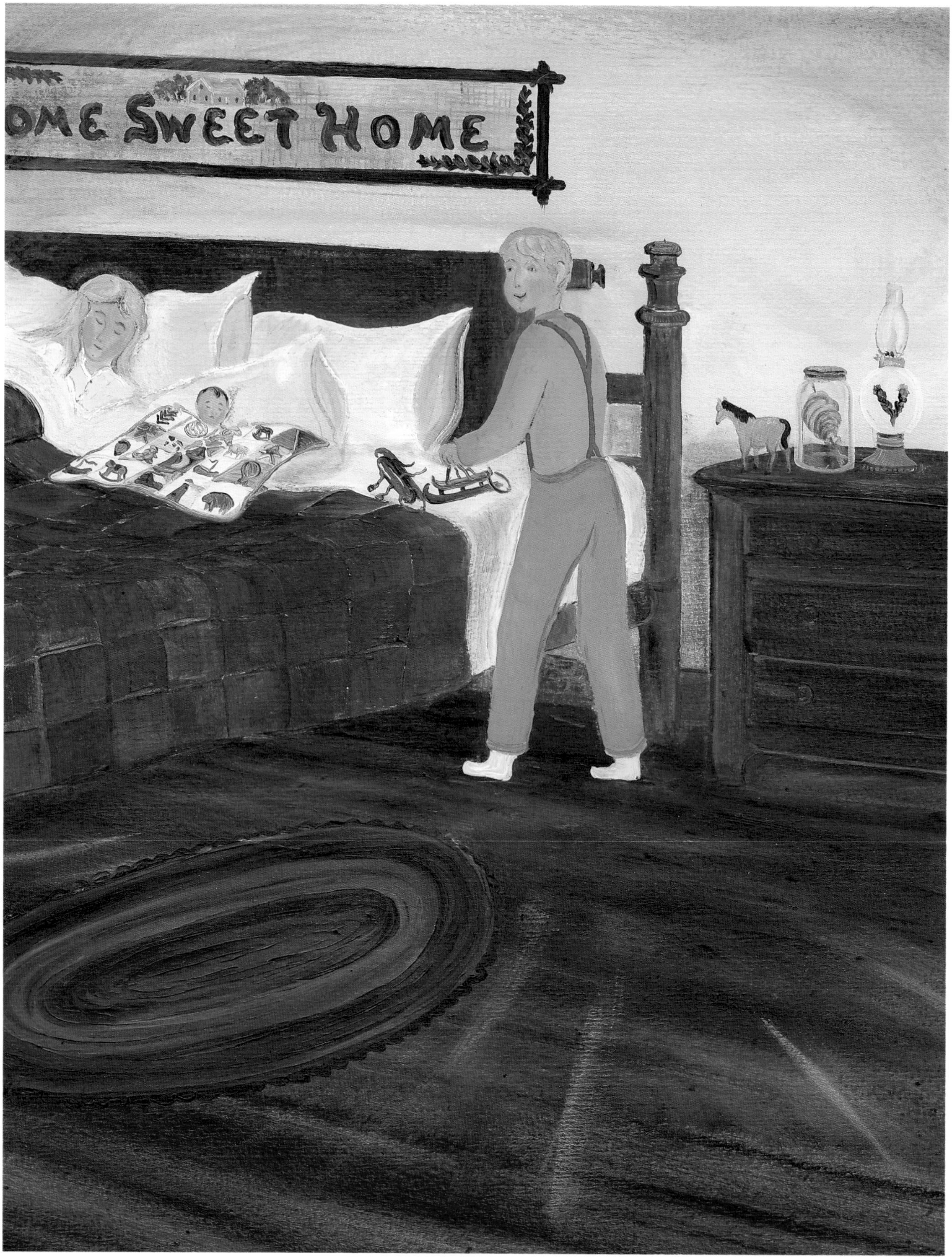
OME SWEET HOME

And there he carefully laid down his precious skates.

"They are too big for you now, baby," he whispered, "but they're a promise. Someday, I'll teach you to skate just like me and Tom Henry. We'll make the fanciest sixes and eights that have ever been seen in this valley."

Now, as children often do, Andy crawled up onto that giant quilt-covered featherbed, lying so close to the baby that he could smell her baby sweetness. And it was right there that Andy fell asleep on that special night. A silent night, when a new baby came to a wintery Vermont valley, where snow clouds hung puffy over the hills and farms, barns, narrow lanes, and skating ponds.

Only now, as Andy closed his eyes
for the night, the stars shone brightly.

# SILENT NIGHT, HOLY NIGHT

Silent night, holy night!
All is calm, all is bright,
Round yon virgin mother and child!
Holy Infant, so tender and mild,
Sleep in heavenly peace,
Sleep in heavenly peace.

Silent night, holy night!
Shepherds quake at the sight,
Glories stream from heaven afar,
Heavenly hosts sing:  "Alleluia;
Christ the Savior is born,
Christ the Savior is born."

Silent night, holy night!

Son of God, love's pure light

Radiant beams from Thy holy face,

With the dawn of redeeming grace,

Jesus, Lord, at Thy birth,

Jesus, Lord, at Thy birth.


Silent night, holy night!

Wondrous star, lend thy light;

With the angels let us sing,

Alleluia to our King;

Christ the Savior is born,

Christ the Savior is born.

For Georgianna Mary Moses

PUFFIN BOOKS
Published by the Penguin Group
Penguin Putnam Books for Young Readers,
345 Hudson Street, New York, New York 10014, U.S.A.
Penguin Books Ltd, 80 Strand, London WC2R ORL, England
Penguin Books Australia Ltd, 250 Camberwell Road, Camberwell, Victoria 3124, Australia
Penguin Books Canada Ltd, 10 Alcorn Avenue, Toronto, Ontario, Canada M4V 3B2
Penguin Books (N.Z.) Ltd, 182-190 Wairau Road, Auckland 10, New Zealand
Penguin Books Ltd, Registered Offices: Harmondsworth, Middlesex, England

First published in the United States of America by Philomel Books,
a division of The Putnam & Grosset Group, 1997
Published by Puffin Books, a division of Penguin Putnam Books for Young Readers, 2002

1 3 5 7 9 10 8 6 4 2

Copyright © Will Moses, 1997
All rights reserved

THE LIBRARY OF CONGRESS HAS CATALOGED THE PHILOMEL EDITION AS FOLLOWS:
Moses, Will.  Silent night / written and illustrated by Will Moses.   p. cm
Summary: One snowy Christmas Eve a Vermont community makes preparations for
the holiday as well as for the arrival of another Christmas miracle.
[1. Christmas—Fiction. 2. Babies—Fiction.]
I. Title.  PZ7.M8477Si  1997[Fic]—dc20  96-18585  CIP  AC
ISBN: 0-399-23100-5 (hc)

Puffin Books ISBN 0-698-11964-9

Printed in United States of America